THOMAS & FRIENDS

SODOR'S
LEGEND
OF THE
LOST TREASURE

Illustrated by Tommy Stubbs

A GOLDEN BOOK • NEW YORK

Thomas the Tank Engine & Friends™

CREATED BY BRITT ALLCROFT

Based on The Railway Series by The Reverend W Awdry.
© 2015 Gullane (Thomas) LLC.
Thomas the Tank Engine & Friends and Thomas & Friends are trademarks of Gullane (Thomas) Limited.
HIT and the HIT Entertainment logo are trademarks of HIT Entertainment Limited.
All rights reserved. Published in the United States by Golden Books, an imprint of Random House
Children's Books, a division of Penguin Random House LLC, 1745 Broadway, New York, NY 10019, and
in Canada by Random House of Canada, a division of Penguin Random House Ltd., Toronto. Golden
Books, A Golden Book, A Little Golden Book, the G colophon, and the distinctive gold spine are registered
trademarks of Penguin Random House LLC.
ISBN 978-0-553-52074-3 (trade) — ISBN 978-0-553-52075-0 (ebook)
randomhousekids.com   www.thomasandfriends.com
Printed in the United States of America
10 9 8 7 6 5 4 3 2 1
Random House Children's Books supports the First Amendment and celebrates the right to read.

It was a sunny day on the Island of Sodor. "A perfect day," Thomas thought, "for racing Bertie."

"You know that Sir Topham Hatt doesn't approve of you racing," Annie said.

"Nonsense! I'll always be Sir Topham Hatt's number one engine," Thomas puffed.

Thomas raced past Gordon, pulling the coaches faster and faster—until he reached a red signal.

Thomas gasped as he came to a sudden stop. The coaches flew off the tracks!

Sir Topham Hatt was not happy when he heard what Thomas had done. He told Thomas to work on the new branch line.

"What about *my* branch line?" Thomas peeped.

A new engine named Ryan rolled up. "I will look after that branch line."

Thomas went to work on the new branch line.
But he didn't pay attention to the danger signs.
Suddenly, the earth crumbled away beneath him.

Thomas crashed down into a giant
underground cavern.

Thomas saw something amazing. An old
pirate ship!

Rocky pulled the pirate ship up out of the cavern. All the engines wanted to see the buried ship.

"If there's a buried pirate ship, there must be buried treasure, too!" Marion peeped. She made a wish that she would dig up the treasure.

Not far off, a mysterious sailor stood in his sailboat.

"Stop bobbing about," he commanded.

"Sorry," the boat replied. The sailor raised his telescope to watch work on the new branch line. He started to make a plan.

That night, Thomas went to the sheds to rest, but Ryan was already there. He invited Thomas in, but Thomas was feeling upset.

Thomas rolled away into the night. Then he saw a ghost boat glowing in the dark!

Thomas followed the eerie sailboat. A ghostly
figure stood on its deck. It glided up to the edge
of the hole that led into the cavern.

That's when Thomas realized it wasn't a
ghost boat. "He's got wheels!"

Thomas introduced himself.

"My name is Sailor John," the man said.

"And I'm Skiff," the boat said. "We're looking for treasure."

Sailor John tied a rope around his waist, and

DANGER AHEAD

DAN
AHE

Thomas lowered him into the cavern.

"I've found it!" Sailor John exclaimed from the hole.

"The treasure?!" Thomas asked.

"No," the sailor called back. "The map!"

The sun was rising as Thomas returned to the new branch line.

He saw Ryan go to an old hopper to fill up with coal. Thomas knew it was bad coal, but he didn't say anything.

Ryan went to fetch some dynamite. His funnel was spitting sparks because of the bad coal. The trucks with the dynamite caught on fire!

Thomas pushed the flaming trucks away. They rolled into the giant cavern. The dynamite exploded with a mighty *kaboom!*

Sir Topham Hatt was very upset. He sent
Thomas to a siding for the rest of the day.
In the afternoon, Marion's shovel uncovered
a treasure chest. Her wish had come true!

Sailor John was angry. "I haven't searched all this time for someone else to find that treasure!" he growled.

Skiff was confused. "You always said we would give it to a museum."

Thomas returned to the new branch line.
Ryan rolled up next to him.

"I'm sorry you got in trouble," Ryan peeped.

"I should be the one saying sorry," Thomas
replied. "I should have warned you about the
bad coal."

That night, Thomas hid behind some sheds, near where the treasure was stored. While he waited, he fell asleep.

Skiff and Sailor John rolled up to the platform. Sailor John snuck into the office and stole the treasure.

"Help!" Skiff cried. "Help!"

Thomas woke and started to chase them.

Thomas raced as fast as he could. His
whistle blew a warning to all the nearby trains.
"Thomas!" Skiff shouted. "Run me off the
rails! I won't mind."

Thomas sped up and bumped Skiff. The tiny
boat splashed into the harbor.
Thomas couldn't stop. He leaped off the rails
and fell into the surf.

"The treasure is too heavy!" Skiff cried. "Throw it overboard or we'll be sunk."

"No!" shouted Sailor John.

Skiff knocked Sailor John into the water. The treasure toppled over, too. It sank.

The police soon arrived and took Sailor John away.

Divers rescued the treasure and delivered it to the museum just in time for the opening of the new branch line.

"My engines are much more important to me than any treasure!" Sir Topham Hatt said. "And you, Thomas, are my number one."